Three Young Knights

Annie Hamilton Donnell

Contents

THREE YOUNG KNIGHTS

BY

Annie Hamilton Donnell

CHAPTER I.

The last wisp of hay was in the Eddy mows. "Come on!" shouted Jot. "Here she goes--hip, hip, hoo-ray!"

"Hoor-a-ay!" echoed Kent. But of course Old Tilly took it calmly. He planted his brown hands pocket-deep and his bare, brown legs wide apart, and surveyed the splendid, bursting mows with honest pride.

"Yes, sir, that's the finest lot o' hay in Hexham county; beat it if you can, sir!" he said approvingly. Then, being ready, he caught off his own hat and cheered, too.

"Hold on, you chaps; give the old man a chance to holler with you!" Father Eddy's big, hearty voice cried above the din, and there was the flaring, sun-browned "wide-awake" swinging with the other hats.

"Hooray for the best hay in town! Hooray for the smartest team o' boys! Hooray for lib-er-tee!"

"Hooray! Hooray!"

They were all of them out of breath and red in the face, but how they cheered! Liberty--that was something to cheer for! After planting-time and haying, hurrah for liberty!

The din softened gradually. With a sweep of his arm, father gathered all the boys in a laughing heap before him.

"Well," he said, "what next? Who's going to celebrate? I'm done with you for a fortnight. I'm going to hire Esau Whalley to milk and do the chores, and send you small chaps about your business. You've earned your holiday. And I don't know but it's as good a time as any to settle up. Pay day's as good one day as another."

He drew out a little tight roll of bills and sorted out three five-dollar notes gravely. The boys' eyes began to shine. Father 'most always paid them, after haying, but--five dollars apiece! Old Tilly pursed his lips and whistled softly. Kent nudged Jot.

[Illustration: He sorted out three five-dollar notes gravely.]

"There you are! You needn't mind about giving receipts!" Father Eddy said matter-of-factly, but his gray eyes were a-twinkle under their cliffs of gray brows. He was exulting quietly in the delight he could read in the three round, brown faces. Good boys--yes, sir--all of them! Wasn't their beat in Hexham county--no, sir! Nor yet in Marylebone county or Winnipeg!

"Now, on with you--scatter!" he laughed. "Mother and I are going to mill to celebrate! When you've decided what you're going to do, send a committee o' three to let us know. Mind, you can celebrate any way you want to that's sensible."

The boys waited till the tall, stoop-shouldered figure had gone back into the dim, hay-scented barn, then with one accord the din began again.

"Hoo-ray! Hoo-ray for father!"

"Father! father! hoo-ray!"

"Hoor-a-ay!"

It died away, began again, then trailed out to a faint wail as the boys scuttled off round the barn to the orchard. Father smiled to himself unsteadily.

"Good boys! good boys! good boys!" he muttered.

"Come on up in the consultery!" cried Kent excitedly.

"Yes, come on, Old Till; that's the place!" Jot echoed.

The "consultery" was a platform up in the great horse-chestnut tree. When there was time, it could be reached comfortably by a short ladder, but, in times of hurry, it was the custom to swing up to it by a low-hanging bough, with a long running jump as a starter. To-day they all swung up.

"Oh, I say, won't there be times!" cried Kent. "Five apiece is fifteen, lumped. You can celebrate like everything with fifteen dollars!"

"Sure--but how?" Old Tilly asked in his gentle, moderate way. "We don't want any old, common celebration!"

"You better believe we don't!"

"No, sir, we want to do something new! Camping out's old!"

"Camping's no good! Go on!" Jot said briefly. It was always Old Tilly they looked to for suggestions. If you waited long enough, they were sure to come.

"Well, that's the trouble. I can't 'go on'--yet. You don't give a chap time to wink! What we want is to settle right down to it and think out a fine way to celebrate. It's got to take time."

For the space of a minute it was still in the consultery, save for the soft swish of the leaves overhead and roundabout. Then Jot broke out--a minute was Jot's utmost limit of silence.

"We could go up through the Notch and back, you know," he reflected. "That's no end of fun. Wouldn't cost us all more'n a fiver for the round trip, and we'd have the other ten to--to--"

"Buy popcorn and 'Twin Mountain Views' with!" finished Kent in scorn. "Well, if you want to dress up in your best fixin's and stew all day in a railroad train--"

"I don't!" rejoined Jot, hastily. "I was thinking of Old Till!"

Tilly's other name was Nathan, but it had grown musty with disuse. He was the oldest of the Eddy trio, and "ballasted" the other two, Father Eddy said. Old Tilly was fourteen and the Eddy twins--Jotham and Kennet--were twelve. All three were well-grown, lusty fellows who could work or celebrate their liberty, as the case might be, with a good will. Just now it was the latter they wanted to do, in some untried way.

It was a beautiful thinking-place, up in the consultery. The birds in the meshes of leaves that roofed it over twittered in whispers, as if they realized that a momentous question was under consultation down below and bird-courtesy demanded quiet.

Jot fretted impatiently under his breath,

"Shouldn't think it need to take all day!" he muttered. "You're as slow as--as--"

"Old Tilly!" laughed Kent. The spell of silence was broken, and the birds overhead broke into jubilant trills, as if they were laughing, too.

"I guess the name fits all right this time," Old Tilly said ruefully. "I can't seem to think of anything at all! My head clicks--the mowing machine wheels have got into it, I guess!"

"Wheels in mine, too!" Kent drawled lazily.

"Wheels!"

Jot sprang to his feet in excitement. In his haste he miscalculated the dimensions of the consultery. There was a wild flutter of brown hands and feet, and then the chestnut leaves closed calmly over the opening, and there were but two boys in the consultery. One of those parted the leaves again and peered down.

"Hello, Jot!"

No answer. Old Tilly's laugh froze on his face.

"Jot! Hello!" he cried, preparing to swing himself down.

"Hello yourself!" came up calmly.

"Oh! Are you killed?"

"'Course! But, I say, you needn't either o' you sit up there any longer gloomin'. I've thought of the way we'll celebrate. It's great!"

The crisp branches creaked as the others swung down to the ground in haste.

"You haven't!" cried Kent.

"What is it, quick!" Old Tilly said. Old Tilly in a hurry!

"Wheels!" announced Jot, deliberately. "You chaps had 'em in your head, and that put 'em into mine. Yes, sir, we'll celebrate on wheels!"

"Why, of course! Good for you!" shouted Kent. But Old Tilly weighed things first in his mind.

"That would be a go if we had enough to 'go' round. But you twinnies wouid have to ride double, or spell each other, or something."

"Spell nobody!" scornfully cried Jot.

"N-o, no, b-o-d--"

"Shut up, Kent! That's all right, Old Till. Benny Tweed'll lend me his bike just like a book--I know Ben! Besides, he owes me a dollar and I'll call it square. There!"

Old Tilly nodded approvingly. "Good!" he said. "Then we'll take a trip off somewhere. That what you meant?"

"Sure! We'll go Columbus-ing--discovering things, you know."

"Like those fellows--what's their names?--who did errands for people, and had wonderful things happen to them while doing them!" put in Kent, enthusiastically.

"Errands? What in the world--knights? He means knight-errants!" exclaimed Old Till, laughing.

"That's a good one--'Did errands for folks!'" Jot mocked.

"Well, what did they do then, Jotham Eddy?"

"Why, they--er--they--they rode round on splendid horses, all armed-- er-- aaple-pie--and--"

"Apple-pie--armed with apple-pie!"

Old Tilly came briskly to the rescue.

"Never mind the errands or the pie!" laughed he. "We'll be reg'lar knights and hunt up distressed folks to relieve, and have reg'lar adventures. It will be great-- good for Jot! We won't decide where we're going or anything--just keep a-going. We'll start to-morrow morning at sunrise."

"Hoo-ray for to-morrow morning!"

"Hoo-ray for sunrise!"

"Hoo-ray for Jot!" finished Kent, generously forgetting mockeries.

The plan promised gloriously. When father and mother came home from the mill they fell in with it heartily, and mother rolled up her sleeves at once to make cakes to fill the boys' bundle racks. They would buy other things as they went along--that would be part of the fun.

In the middle of the night Jot got out of bed softly and padded his way across to the bureau, to feel of the three five-dollar bills they had left together under the pincushion for a paper weight. He slid his fingers under carefully. What! He lifted the cushion. Then he struck a match--two matches--three, in agitated succession.

The money was gone!

CHAPTER II.

Jot gasped with horror. The last match went out and left him standing there in the dark. After one instant's hesitation he made a bound for the bed. "Kent! Kent! Wake up!" he whispered shrilly. He shook the limp figure hard.

"Thieves! Murder! Wake up, I tell you, Kent! We're robbed!"

"M-m--who's rob--Oh, say, lemme alone!" murmured poor Kent, drowsily. Jot shook him again.

"I tell you thieves!" he hissed in his ear. "The money's gone! Do you hear? It isn't under the pin-cushion where we left it! It's gone! We've been robbed, Kent Eddy!"

The limp figure strengthened as if electrified and rose to a sitting position. Kent's eyes flew open.

"What?" he cried.

"Get up quick, Kentie, and we'll wake Old Tilly up! Maybe we can catch 'em!"

"Catch who? I wish you'd talk English, Jot Eddy!"

Old Tilly was slumbering peacefully, oblivious to thieves and five-dollar bills alike. It took a long time to wake him and longer yet to make him understand the dire thing that had happened.

"Get up! Get up! We've got to catch 'em!" concluded Jot.

"Yes, the thieves--catch the thieves, you know!" Kent explained. "I don't s'pose you'll lie there all night and let 'em cut off with our money, if you are Old Tilly!"

Then something funny happened. Anyway, it seemed funny to Old Tilly. He buried his face in the pillow and choked with laughter.

"It's gone to his head!" whispered Jot, in alarm.

"No, to his t-toe!" giggled Old Tilly, purple in the face.

"Yes, sir, he's crazy as a loon. Let's call father, Jot!"

"Hold on!--wait! It's all right, boys! The money is, and I am, and everybody is! Just wait till I get my laugh out, won't you?"

"No, sir, but we'll wait till you get out o' bed and that's this very minute!" Jot exclaimed wrathfully. He was dancing up and down with impatience.

Old Tilly slowly brought a lean, shapely leg into view from beneath the sheet. To the boys' amazement it was covered with a long black stocking. Old Tilly, like the other boys, had been barefooted all day.

"Thought I might as well get a good start in dressing!" he chuckled. "Nothing like being read--"

"Oh, come off!"

"Well, I wish it would; there's something in the toe that hurts. Ow!"

He drew off the stocking and gravely examined the snug little wad in the toe.

"The money!" cried Kent.

"Yes, sir, the money!" Jot echoed in astonishment.

"Why, so it is!" Old Tilly said in evident surprise. "Then the thieves didn't get away with it, after all! I call that a lucky stroke--my getting partly dressed over-night! No, hold on, you little chaps--don't get uppy! I'll explain, honest I will! You see, I got up after a while and put the money there for safe-keeping. I'd like to see the thief that would look there for it! He'd get a good kick if he did!"

It was half an hour later when the trio settled back into sleep again. In the east already there were dim outriders of day trailing across the darkness.

Without further incident the three knights-errant got under way next day. In a glare of July sunshine they rode away in search of adventures, while Father and Mother Eddy in the kitchen doorway looked after them a little wistfully.

"Bless their hearts!" mother murmured tender-wise.

"Good boys! Good boys!" said father, coughing to cover the break in his voice.

"I say, this is great!" called Jot, who led the van, of course. "This is the way to do it!"

[Illustration: "I say, this is great!" called Jot.]

"Yes, sir!" Kent cried in high feather, "it feels as if you were reg'lar old knights, you know! Isn't it jolly not to know what's going to happen next?"

Old Tilly's wheel slid up abreast of Kent's and proceeded sociably.

"Esau Whalley's farm 'happens next,' and then old Uncle Rod King's next," Old

Tilly said calmly. "I guess we better wait till we get out o' this neck o' woods before we settle down to making believe!"

But three wheels driven by three pairs of sturdy, well-muscled legs get over miles swiftly, and by ten o'clock the boys had turned down an unfamiliar road and were on the way to things that happened. Before noon knightly deeds were at their hand. Jot himself discovered the first one. He vaulted from his bicycle suddenly, as they were bowling past a little gray house set in weeds, and the others, looking back, saw him carrying a dripping pail of water along the path to the kitchen door-steps.

"The pail was out there on the well curb, asking to be filled," he explained brusquely, as he caught up with them, "and the old woman pumping into it didn't look as if lugging water agreed with her. Besides, I wanted a drink."

"You didn't get one," retorted Kent, wisely.

Jot cast a sidewise glance upon him.

"I said I wanted one, didn't I? Anybody can want a drink."

"And take your remedy. Dose: lug one pail o' water for an old woman. If not successful, repeat in ten min--"

Jot made a rapid spurt and left his teaser behind. When Old Tilly had come abreast of him again, he reached out a brotherly hand and bestowed a hearty pat on his arm.

"Good boy!" he said, and unconsciously his voice was like father's, miles back in the kitchen doorway. It was the way father would have said it.

"That's the way to do. We'll pick up 'errands' to do for folks. What's the use of being knights?"

And Old Tilly's turn came next, in the way of driving the cows out of somebody's corn patch and propping up the broken fence. If it took but a few minutes, what of that? It saved a bent old man's rheumatic leg's, and the gay whistle that went with it drifted into an open window and pleased a little fretful child.

"My turn next!" shouted Kent, gliding away from them out of sight over the brow of a hill.

"Good luck to you!" called Jot. "We're going into camp to take a bite. No use being in such a rush."

"When you come my way, drop in!" floated back faintly. They tilted their wheels against trees and threw themselves down in the shade to rest. Jot was ravenous with hunger.

"Cakes are all right to begin on," he said, regarding mother's bountiful store with approval. "But when I strike the next store you'll see the crackers and cheese fly!"

"I don't mind taking a hand in the scrimmage myself!" laughed Old Tilly, munching a fat cake. "I say, wasn't Kent foolish to go scooting off like that? Might as well have begun easy. I move we ride nights and mornings mostly, and loaf noons. There's a moon, 'silver mo-oo-on'--"

His voice trailed lazily into song. It was pleasant lounging in the shade and remembering the hay was all in and adventures ahead.

An hour or so later they moved on at a leisurely pace, looking for Kent. The general direction had been agreed upon, so they experienced no anxiety. It added to the fun to hunt for him.

"Where in the world did he go to?" queried Old Tilly, laughing. "He disappeared like a streak of lightning!"

"I see him--there, under that tree!" cried Jot, waving a salute. "He's lying down and enjoying life."

But it was a tired old man under the tree, and, from his forlorn face, he did not seem to be "enjoying life." He was very old, very shabby, very tired. His unkempt figure had collapsed feebly by the way apparently. What astonished the boys was the wheel that lay on its side near him. He did not look like a wheelman.

"Hold on. Old Till, I say!" called Jot in sudden excitement, forging ahead to his side. "I say, that looks like our wheel--mine and Kent's! I guess I know our wheel!"

Jot was riding the borrowed machine. Kent had the one they owned jointly.

"You're right, sonny; it looks that way!" rejoined Old Tilly, excited in his turn. "But we can't pounce on it and cut, you know. How do we know what Kent's up to?"

Jot grunted derisively. "Probably he's given it to the old duffer for a birthday present--hundredth anniversary!" he scoffed. "That would be taking his turn at doing knight-errands. Let's go right on and not disturb the poor old man--"

"Let's have sense!" remarked Old Tilly, briefly. "We'll forge on ahead and hunt

Kent up before we arrest tramps for bike-lifting. When he says he's been robbed it'll be time to holler 'Stop, thief!'"

"Yes, come on!" Jot called back as he shot ahead. "I haven't a doubt but we'll find Kentie's got his bike tucked away all safe in the toe of his stocking!"

They came almost instantly into the outskirts of a snug little settlement. The road was flanked on both sides by neat white houses. Trig little children scurried out of their way, cheering shrilly. Somewhere there was music. [Transcriber's note: the word "trig", above, is as it appears in the original book.]

"Hark!" Jot cried.

"Hark yourself! That's a good hand-organ," Old Tilly said; and he hummed the familiar tune, and both wheels sped on to the time of it, as it seemed. The music grew louder. "Look up in that dooryard, will you! Jot Eddy, look at the chap that's grinding it!"

Jot uttered an exclamation of astonishment.

CHAPTER III.

Up in one of the shady side yards stood Kent, turning the crank of a hand-organ! He was facing the highway where the other two boys were, but not a trace of recognition was in his face. Ranged in a semicircle before him was a line of little children shuffling their toes to the gay tune.

"It's Kent!" gasped Jot.

"Or his ghost--pretty lively one! Where in the world did he get that hand-organ? And what's he done with his bike? Why--oh!"

Old Tilly added two and two, and, in the light of a sudden inspiration, they made four. Yes, of course, that was it, but he would wait and let Jot guess it out for himself. Jot had other business in hand just then.

"Say, come on up there with the youngsters, Old Till!" he whispered excitedly. "Come on, quick! We'll make him smile! He can't keep his face with us tagging on with the children!"

They left their wheels beside the road and stalked solemnly up the path. The children were too intent on the music to notice them, and the figure at the crank did not change its stiff, military attitude. The tune lurched and swayed on.

Suddenly, with a sharp click, the music swept into something majestic and martial, with the tread of soldiers' feet and the boom of drums in it. The faces of the little children grew solemn, and unconsciously their little shoulders straightened and they stood "at attention." They were all little patriots at heart and they longed to step into file and tramp away to that splendid music.

Again the tune changed sharply, and still again. Then the organ-grinder slung his instrument with an experienced twist and twirl across his shoulders, and took off his cap.

"Look, will you? He's going to pass it round!" giggled Jot, under his breath.

"He'll pass it to us, Old Till!"

"Keep your face straight, mind!" commanded Old Till, sharply.

The organ-grinder handed round his cap, up and down the crooked line of his audience. The two sober boys at one end dropped in a number of pennies, one at a time deliberately,

"Bless ye!" murmured the organ-grinder, gratefully. Jot's brown face tweaked with the agony of keeping straight, but Old Tilly was equal to the occasion. He assumed a benevolent, pitying expression.

"Hold on a minute!" he called. "Here's a nickel for your poor wife and children. How many you got?"

"Five, sir, your honor," the musician murmured thickly.

"Starving?"

"Sure--all but a couple of the little uns. They're up 'n' dressed, thank ye; bless ye!"

Jot made a strange, choking sound in his throat.

"Is the young gent took ill?" inquired the organ-grinder, solicitously.

"No, oh, no; only a slight attack of strangulating--he's liable to attacks. It was the music--too much for him!'" Old Tilly gravely explained, but his lips quivered and struggled to smile.

The whole little procession trailed slowly down the lane to the street. At the next house and at all the others in succession, it turned in and arranged itself in line again, prepared to listen with ears and dancing toes. Jot and Old Tilly followed on in the rear. They found it hard work to find pennies enough to drop into the organ-grinder's cap at every round. Toward the end they economized narrowly.

The small settlement came to an abrupt ending just over the brow of the hill. The houses gave out, and the musician and his audience swung about and retraced their steps. The children dropped off, a few at a time, until there were left only the three boys, who went on soberly together.

"Oh, say!" broke out Jot at last.

"'Tis not for the likes o' me to 'say,' your honor," the organ-grinder murmured humbly, and Jot gave him a violent nudge.

"Let's knock off foolin'!" he cried. "I say, where'd you get that machine, Kentie? Where'd you get it? And for the sake o' goodness gracious, where's your wheel?"

"'Turn, turn, my wheel,'" quoted Kent from the Fourth Reader. He was shaking with suppressed laughter, that turned into astonishment at Old Tilly's calm rejoinder. If it didn't take Old Till to ferret things out!

"It isn't liable to 'turn, turn,' while that old tramp has it," Tilly said calmly. "He isn't built for a rider. What kind of a trade did you make, anyway? Going halves?"

"No, going wholes!" Kent answered briefly, and would say no more. They went on down the sandy road. When they got back to the forlorn old figure under the tree, it was slowly rising up and regarding them out of tired, lack-luster eyes. The wheel still leaned comfortably in its place close by.

"Me--bring--money. Play--tunes. You--buy--food," Kent said very slowly and distinctly, pausing between every word. "He's a foreigner, you know," he explained over his shoulder to the boys. "He no understand. You have to talk pigeon English to him. See how he catches on to what I said?"

The old face had grown less dull and weary. A slow light seemed to illumine it. As the little stream of pennies dripped into the tremulous, wrinkled old hand, it suddenly flashed into a smile. Then a stream of strange words issued from the old man's lips. They tripped over each other and made weird, indistinguishable combinations of sound, but the boys translated them by the light of that smile. How pleased the old fellow was! How he fingered over the pennies exultantly!

"Tell the whole story, old man," Old Tilly said quietly as they mounted their wheels and glided off. "It looks like a reg'lar novel!"

"Yes, hurry up, can't you!" impatiently Jot urged. "Begin at the beginning, and go clear through to the end."

"You've helped folks. Why shouldn't I? There weren't any old ladies with empty water pails, or any cows in corn lots, so I had to take up with the poor old organ-grinder. That's all."

"All!" scoffed Jot, "Go on with the rest of it, Kent Eddy!"

"Isn't any 'rest,'" grunted Kent, "unless you count the organ-grinder; he had some-looked as if he'd rested. Well, sir"--Kent suddenly woke up--"but without any fooling, you ought to have seen that old chap when I came on him. He was all used up--heat, you know. There was a creek, back a ways, and the water kind of pulled him up. He couldn't talk English, but he offered me a black two-cent piece for pay. He turned his pocket out to find it. That set me to thinking I'd make him a little richer."

"Of course! Go on!" hurried Jot.

"Isn't any 'on.'"

"There's honor," Old Tilly cried softly. "I say that was splendid, Kentie! I like that!"

Kent flushed uneasily. Old Tilly's face looked like father's when he said his rare, hearty words of commendation.

"Well, the organ-grinder likes it, too!" Kent laughed. "Now he can have something to eat. Poor old fellow! He couldn't have gone through all those dooryards to save his life! He was 'most sunstruck. I told a motherly old lady about him, at one of the houses, and she's going to be on the lookout for him, and give him a snack of meat and bread."

They went on for half a mile quite silently. Then, without warning. Jot suddenly began to laugh. He tumbled off his bicycle and collapsed in a feeble heap.

"Don't anybody st-op me !" he cried. "It's dangerous! I'm having one o' my 'attacks'!"

The others joined in, and, for a little, the woods rang with boyish mirth.

"It was rich!" stammered Jot. "Passing the hat round capped it!"

"It was great!" laughed Old Tilly. "You're an actor, Kentie!"

"Me! What are you?"

"Well, I can't grind a hand-organ and pass round the hat like that!"

"I could!" Jot cried, suddenly sobering down and going through the motions of turning a crank with airy ease. "It's 'most too easy for me!"

The fun lasted until night. It was Saturday, and they rode until sunset without further stops.

"We'll rest awhile and then go on by moonlight," Old Tilly said. "It will be jolly and cool then. Besides, we don't want to be on the road to-morrow. I promised mother I'd see that you all kept Sunday."

"And go to church ?" Jot said.

"Yes, and go to church, it there's one to go to anywhere," Old Tilly rejoined quietly. "I told mother I'd see that you fellows went to church quiet and nice, if possible. She put in the extra collars and neckties on purpose."

A long rest, with a hearty lunch, and then they were off again in the clear moonlight. It was splendid. The trees, the road, the pale, ghostly houses--everything had a weird, charmed aspect. They might have been riding through fairyland. It was growing late, they knew, and at last they stopped, out of sheer weariness.

A great, square bulk loomed faintly before them in the waning moonlight. It might be a house--might be a mountain! Jot spurted on ahead to reconnoiter.

"House!" he shouted back. "Doors open--all quiet--guess it's on a picnic ground. I felt a stair that seemed to lead up to a balcony or something."

"Well, we're sleepy enough. We'll take anything we can get!" yawned Kent. "Come on, then."

And, riding into what seemed a yard, they found a good place for their wheels under some bushes. The moon was too low to give them any light, but the boys found the doorway to the big building and went up the stairs, guided by their hands along the narrow passageway. They could only discern a queer little enclosure, topped by a little rail. They were too thoroughly tired out to be curious, and, feeling some narrow seats, they lay down, and, making themselves comfortable, were soon asleep.

Jot was dreaming that Old Tilly had made him go to church and the people were singing, when suddenly he opened his eyes. Was he dreaming? Over him floated a sweet hymn, one his mother loved to join in singing at church Sunday morning. The boy's eyes opened wider still at sight of flecks of sunshine dancing on the walls near, and, raising his head, he saw through the clear little panes of a long window, where the green leaves were dancing against the glass. The singing went on, and the boy raised himself in a wondering fashion upon his elbow. Where were they? Jot lifted his head still higher, and, glancing over the railing, he looked down upon a goodly company. The amazement on his face grew greater instead of less. They were in church!--that was sure.   Jot looked back to his sleeping companions and held his breath as one of them stirred uneasily. What if he should roll off the bench?   The hymn grew louder and sweeter, and Jot smoothed out his hair and straightened his necktie and sat up straight. The branches outside tapped the narrow, small paned window near him, and from the open windows below the sweet beauty of the summer morning stole in. But as the minister rose to give out his text, a sound from one of the boys back of him caused Jot to turn.

CHAPTER IV.

Jot turned in his narrow seat there in the church gallery as he heard a sound that made him think his brothers were waking. But Old Tilly had only stirred in his sleep and struck out a little jarringly against the back of the narrow gallery pew. Jot turned back and scanned the place they had so innocently taken for their quarters the night before. The gallery pew they were in was like a tiny half-walled room, with seats running around three sides and up to the queer door on the fourth side. The walls of the pews were almost as high as Jot's head if he had dared to stand up.

Kent stirred uneasily and threw out his arm with a smart rap against the side. Jot crept across to him in terror. "Sh! Sh! Keep quiet! don't breathe! You're in meeting!" he whispered. "The minister's down there preaching now! Oh, sh!"

"Lemme--" But Jot's hand cut off the rest. The other hand gently shook Kent's arm.

"I tell you we're in meeting; don't make a sound!"

"Who's making a sound?" whispered Kent, now thoroughly awake. Was Jot taken suddenly crazy? Hark! who was that talking?

"If you don't believe me, raise your eye over that wall and sec what!" whispered Jot eagerly. He drew Kent up beside him and they peeped carefully over. Kent dropped back, as Jot had done, in sheer surprise. The two boys gazed at each other silently. It was too much for Kent, though, and, to suppress a laugh, he stuffed his handkerchief in his mouth.

Kent pointed to Old Tilly and smiled broadly.

"He promised mother he'd take us to meeting," he whispered, "and he's done it!"

"Yes, but she wouldn't like to see him asleep in church!" Jot whispered hack.

Below them the minister's deep voice tolled on solemnly. They could not catch all the words.

"Come on! I'm going to sit up like folks. I want to hear what he's saying," Jot whispered after awhile.

They smoothed their hair and tried to straighten collars and ties, and then suddenly some of the people down below in the body of the church glanced up and saw two boyish faces, side by side, in the gallery. The puzzle was beyond unraveling. The women prodded each other gently with their parasol tips and raised their eyebrows. The men looked blank. When had those youngsters got up there in that pew? One of the deacons scowled a little, but the two quiet brown faces allayed his suspicions. It wasn't mischief--it was mystery.

The sight that had met Jot's astonished eyes in the beginning was a quaint one. This was a new kind of a church! At home there were rows upon rows of red-cushioned seats, with the hymn books and fans in the racks making the only break to the monotony. Here the pews were all little square rooms with high partitions and doors. The hard board seats ran 'way round them all, so that in some of them people were sitting directly "back to" the minister! Rows on rows of the little rooms, like cells, jutted against each other and filled up the entire space below save the aisles and the pulpit.

[Illustration: This was a new kind of church.]

And the pulpit! Jot's eyes returned to it constantly in wondering admiration. There was a steep flight of stairs leading up to it on each side, and an enormous umbrella-like sounding-board was poised heavily above it. The pulpit itself was round and tail and hung above the heads of the congregation, making the practice of looking up at the good old minister a neck-aching process. Directly beneath the pulpit was a seat facing the people. It was empty now, but a hundred years ago, had the lads but known it, the deacons had sat there and the "tithing-man," whose duty it was to go about waking up the dozers with his long wand. It was called the Deacon's Seat, and if sometimes the deacons themselves had dropped off into peaceful naps--what then? Did the "tithing-man" nudge them sharply with his stick, or was he dozing, too?

There are still a few of these old landmarks left in the country. Now and then we run across them and get a distinct flavor of old times, and it is worth going a good many miles to see the inside of one of them. By just shutting one's eyes and "making believe" a little, how easy it would be to conjure up our dear old grandmothers in their great scoop bonnets, and grandfathers with their high coat collars coming nearly to their bald crowns! And the Deacon's Seat under the pulpit--how easy to make believe the deacons in claw-hammer coats and queer frilled shirt bosoms!

The people Jot and Kent saw were ordinary, modern people, and their modern clothes looked oddly out of date against the quaint old setting. Jot thought with a twinge of sympathy how hard the seats must feel, and how shoulders must ache against the perfectly straight-up-and-down backs. He felt a sudden pity for his great-grandmother and great-uncles and aunts.

This especial old church, box-like and unchurchly without and ancient within, was rarely used for worship except in the summer months. Then there were services in it as often as a minister could be found to conduct them. The three young adventurers had stumbled upon it in the dark and overslept out of sheer physical weariness. It was up in one of the old choir pews in the high gallery they had wakened--or Jot had wakened--to the strains of the beautiful hymn his mother loved.

The whole explanation was simple enough when it was explained. Kent and Jot worked it out slowly in their own minds.

Meanwhile Old Tilly slept on, and the sermon came to an end. There was another hymn and then the benediction. The people dispersed slowly, and once more the big house was deserted.

Then Jot woke Old Tilly. "I say," he cried, "I say, old fellow, wake up!"

"Yes, I'm coming in a minute!" muttered Old Tilly.

"You'll be late for church," remarked Kent dryly, with a wink at Jot.

Old Tilly stirred and rose on his elbow. Then he gave a bewildered look around him.

"You're in church. Didn't you promise mother you'd take us to church?"
"Yes."

"But you slept all through the service," said Kent, "and I shall tell mother so!"

"Kent Eddy, what are you trying to get at? How did we get here, anyhow?" said Old Tilly, rising cautiously; and then, as he looked down on the empty room below, standing to his full height, he said. "Well, if I ever!" a laugh breaking through his white teeth. "I should say we had been in church!" he added. "Why didn't you fellows wake me up? What did the folks think?"

"Oh, they only saw the two good boys sitting on the seat facing them! We didn't say we had another one smuggled in under beside us. But my! You did rap the seat awfully once with your elbow!"

"Well, I know one thing: my shoulder aches from lying on that narrow seat so long," said Old Tilly. "I say, let's go down to the wheels and the grub. I'm half starved!"

"All right," said Kent in rather a subdued way. The morning service had stolen pleasingly through him, and somehow it seemed to the little lad as though their ship had been guided into a wonderfully quiet harbor. And now he followed his brothers down the narrow stairs that they had so innocently groped their way up in darkness the night before. The three had agreed to leave the church and partake of the lunch that was in the baskets on the wheels, but now they found doing so not as easy of accomplishment as they had at first thought. When they tried the outer door they found to their dismay that it was locked. Old Tilly would not believe Kent, and he pushed the latter's hand off the door knob rather impatiently. "Let me get hold of it!"

But, rattle the door as he might, he could not stir the rusty lock.

"Well, we're locked in, that's sure!" said Kent, looking almost dismayed.

CHAPTER V.

"I guess you're right, Jotham," Old Tilly said.

"But what in the world did they go and lock up for, when we got in just as easy as pie last night?" exclaimed Kent, disgustedly.

"Oh, ask something easy!" Jot cried. "What I want to know is, how we're going to get on the other side o' that door."

The care-taker, if one could call him that, of the old meeting-house, had taken it into his head to take care of it!--or it may have been that the key chanced to be in his pocket, convenient. At all events, the door was securely fastened. The three boys reluctantly gave up the attempt to force it.

"Windows!" Kent suddenly exclaimed, and they all laughed foolishly. They had not thought of the windows.

"That's a good joke on the Eddy boys!" Old Tilly said. "We sha'n't hear the last of it if anybody lets on to father."

"Better wait till we're on the other side of the windows!" advised Kent. "Maybe it isn't a joke."

There were windows enough. They were ranged in monotonous rows on all sides of the church, above and below. They all had tiny old-fashioned panes of glass and were fastened with wooden buttons. It was the work of a minute to "unbutton" one of them and jump out.

"There!" breathed Jot in relief, as his toes touched sod again, "I feel as if I'd been in prison and just got out."

"Broken out--that's the way I feel. I wish we could fasten the window again," Old Tilly said thoughtfully.

Kent was rubbing his ankle ruefully.

"It was a joke on us, our mooning round that door all that time, and thinking we were trapped!"

"Oh, well, come on; it doesn't matter, now we're free again."

"Come along--here are our wheels all right," Old Tilly said briskly. "Let's go down to that little bunch of white houses there under the hill, and pick out the one we want to stay over night in."

"The one that wants us to stay in it, you mean! Come on, then."

It was already mid-afternoon. The beautiful Sunday peace that broods over New England's country places rested softly on new-mown fields and bits of pasture and woods. The boys' hearts were made tender by the service they had so unexpectedly attended, and as the beauty of the scene recalled again the home fields, they fell into silence. A tiny, brown-coated bird tilted on a twig and sang to them as they passed. The little throat throbbed and pulsated with eager melody.

Old Tilly listened to the song to its close, then swung round suddenly. His face was like father's when he got up from his knees at family prayers.

"That bird seems singing, 'Holy, holy, holy,'" Old Tilly said softly. "Can't you hear?"

"Yes, I hear," murmured Jot.

The little white house they picked out sat back from the highway in a nest of lilac bushes. It reminded the boys a very little of home.

"Stop over night? Away from home, be ye? Why, yes, I guess me an' pa can take you in. One, two--dear land! there's three of ye, ain't there? Yes, yes, come right in! I couldn't turn three boys away--not three!"

The sweet-faced old woman in the doorway held out both hands welcomingly. She seemed to get at the history of the three young knights by some instinctive mind-reading of her own--the boys themselves said so little. It was the little old lady's sweet voice that ran on without periods, piecing Old Tilly's brief explanatory words together skillfully.

"Havin' a holiday, be you? I see. Well, young folks has to have their outin's. When they git as old as me an' pa, they'll be all innin's!" she ran on. Suddenly she stooped and surveyed them with a placid attempt at sternness. "I hope you've all be'n to meetin'?" she cried.

Jot's face twisted oddly.

"Yes," Old Tilly answered, subduedly, "we've been to church."

"I thought so--I thought so. Now come in an' see pa--poor pa' He was took again yesterday. He's frettin' dretfully about the hay. Pa--"

Her voice went on ahead and heralded their coming. "Here's three boys come to stop over night with us--three, pa. You're glad there's three of 'em, ain't you? I knew you'd be. When I'd counted 'em up, I didn't hesitate any longer! The littlest one looks a little mite like our Joey, pa--only Joey was handsome," she added innocently.

Kent nudged Jot delightedly. They were entering a quaint, old-fashioned room, and at the further end on a hair-cloth settle lay a withered morsel of an old man. His sun-browned face made a shriveled spot of color against the pillows.

"That's pa," the little old lady said, by way of introduction. "He was took yesterday, out in the field. It was dretful hot--an' the hay 'most in, too. He's frettin' because he couldn't 've waited a little mite longer, ain't you, pa? I tell him if the boys was here--" She broke off with a quiver in her thin, clear voice. Pa, on the couch, put out his hand feebly and smoothed her skirt.

"We had three boys--ma an' me," he explained quietly. "That's why ma was so quick to take you in, I guess. They was all little shavers like you be."

"Yes, jest little shavers," said ma, softly. "They hadn't got where I couldn't make over 'em an' tuck 'em in nights, when they was took away-- all in one week. You wouldn't have thought 'twould have be'n all in one week--three boys--would you? Not three! I tell pa the Lord didn't give us time enough to bid 'em all good-by. It takes so long to give up three!"

Old Tilly and the others stood by in odd embarrassment. Jot was bothered with a strange sensation in his throat.

But the old lady's sorrowing face brightened presently. She bustled about the room busily, getting out chairs and setting straight things crooked in her zeal.

"I guess you're hungry, ain't you? Boys always is--an' three boys! Dear! how hungry three boys can be! I'm goin' out to get supper. Pa, you must do the entertainin'."

The bread was "just like mother's"--white with a delicious crust--and the butter yellow as gold, and Jot helped himself plentifully. "Ma," behind the tea urn, watched him with a beaming face.

"That's right!--I love to see boys eat! I tell pa sometimes I can just see our three boys settin' at this table eatin' one of ma's good meals o' victuals. You must have some of this custard, Joey." A faint essence of added tenderness crept into the wistful old voice at that name. The boys knew that Joey had been the little old lady's baby.

"Joey was a great hand for custard. Joey was a master hearty boy."

After supper, the boys wandered out around the tiny farm. It was at best a rocky, uneven place, but there were evidences of "pa's" hard work on it. Most of the grass had been mowed and carried into the barn, but there was one small field still dotted over with cocks of overripe hay. Old Tilly strode over and examined it with an air of wisdom.

"Too ripe," he commented. "I guess it won't be worth getting in, if it stays out here much longer."

"He meant to have it all in yesterday--she said he did. I mean that little old lady said so," Jot remarked.

"Well, if it isn't all in to-morrow, it's a goner," Old Tilly said decisively.

"Now, boys, there's lots o' good water out in the cistern," the old lady said, when they came back. "I've put the towels handy in the shed. It may be you'll sleep sounder if you have a nice sponge off."

Only too glad, the boys took to the shed, and then followed their guide to the airy room waiting. How the pillows fitted a fellow's head! as Jot said luxuriously. And the beds, how good they felt after those hard church pews! They were sound asleep in a moment.

The little old lady stole in to look at them. She held the lamp high in one hand and gazed down with wistful eyes into the three healthy brown faces. When she went back to pa, her face was wet with a rain of tears.

"They look so good, pa, lyin' there!" she said brokenly. "An' you'd ought to see how much like Joey the littlest one throws up his arm!"

The old man could not sleep. He kept asking if it looked like rain and kept fretting because he could not move his legs about freely.

"I've got to move 'em, ma," he groaned.-"I've got to practice before to-morrer, so's to get the hay in. I've got to get the hay in, ma!"

It was Jot, for a wonder, who slept the longest. He woke with a start of surprise at his strange surroundings. Then he sat up in bed, blinking his eyes open wider.

The room was a large one with two beds in it. He and Kent had slept in one, and Old Tilly in the other. It was just before sunrise, and in the east a wide swathe of pink was banding the sky. Outside the window, a crowd of little birds were tuning up for a concert.

Jot rubbed his eyes again. There was no one else in the room. The other boys had vanished completely. He leaped out of bed with a queer sense of fright. Then he made a discovery.

CHAPTER VI.

Come on--haying's begun," the note read. It was in Kent's angular, boyish hand, and Jot found it pinned conspicuously to the looking-glass frame. "Old Till and I are at it. Come on out."

So that was it? They were getting in the poor little morsel of an old man's hay. Jot jumped into his clothes with a leap and was out in the hay-field with them. He was inclined to be cross at being left dozing while the work began.

"I call that shabby mean," he protested. "Why couldn't you wake a fellow up? I guess I'd like a hand in helping the old man out, as well as either of you."

"Wake you up!" laughed Kent. "Didn't I tickle the soles of your feet? Didn't I pinch you? What more do you want?"

"You wouldn't wake up, Jot," Old Tilly said cheerfully. "I took a hand at it myself, but nothing this side of a brass band would 've done it this morning. We couldn't bring that in, you know, for fear of waking the folks. So Kent wrote you a letter."

The work went on splendidly. They were all in fine haying trim, and the cocks in the rough little field were tossed briskly into the rack. There were three loads, and the last one was safely stowed in the haymow before the little old lady in the house had stirred up her breakfast cake.

[Illustration: They were all in fine haying trim.]

"I hope she won't discover anything before we get away," Old Tilly said. "It would be such fun to have it a reg'lar surprise!"

"Wouldn't it!" cried Jot.

"But she might think somebody'd come along in the night and stole it, don't you see?" Kent objected.

"No, sir, I don't see. I guess she'd see our trail. And besides, look up there in the mow! It doesn't look just exactly as it did before we began!"

A few minutes after the boys had glided away on their wheels, the little old lady hurried into "pa's" room.

"Pa, pa, it's all in, jest as nice as a new pin! Every spear's in!" she cried delightedly. "Them three boys did it before breakfast. I knew what they was up to, but I wasn't goin' to spoil their little surprise! I guess I know how boys like surprises. Don't you remember how Hilary an' Eben got the potatoes all dug that time an' surprised you? How innocent their little faces looked when you said, 'Hum-suz-a-day! how it makes my back ache thinkin' o' those potatoes!' Joey was a tittle thing in kilts, but he helped. He tugged 'em in, in his own little basket--I can see jest how proud he looked! But I evened up a little on the surprise. I guess when they come to open them bicycle baskets they'll see some things in the way of apple-pie that was not there earlier!"

All the morning the boys wondered at the stream of wagons traveling their way. Then just at noon they found out what it meant. They came round a sharp curve in the road upon a beautiful grove on the shore of a lake. It was gay with flags and the bright dresses of women and children. Here and there an awning or tent dotted the green spaces. People were bustling about in all directions, laughing and shouting to each other, and every few minutes there were new arrivals.

"Hark! there's a band o' music! It's a circus!" cried Kent, excitedly. Jot had disappeared somewhere in the crowd.

"No-o, not a circus," Old Tilly said doubtfully. "It's some kind of a big picnic. See, there's a kind of a track laid out over there where that flag is. They're going to have some kind of athletics."

"Foot-races and hurdles and things! Oh, I say, can't we stay and see 'em?" Kent cried eagerly.

At that instant appeared Jot, waving his cap in great excitement.

"Come on--we're invited!" he shouted. "There's going to be lots of fun, I tell you! We can buy ice-cream, too, over in that striped tent, and there are boats we can hire to row out in, and--everything."

"Hold on a minute!" demanded Old Tilly with the sternness of authority. "How did you get your invitation? and what is it that's going on, anyway?"

"Tell quick, Jot--hurry! They're getting ready for a foot-race," fidgeted Kent.

"It's a Grangers' picnic, that's what. And a big jolly Granger invited us to stop to it. He asked if we weren't farmer boys, and said he thought so by our cut when I said, yes sir-ee. He wants us to stop. He said so. He says his folks have got bushels of truck for dinner, and we can join in with them and welcome."

"And thanking him kindly, I'll stop!" laughed Kent, in high feather. "Come on over there, Jot, and see 'em race." And the three young knights were presently in the midst of the gay crowd, as gay as anybody.

The afternoon was full of fun for them. They made plenty of acquaintances among the other brown-faced farmer boys, and entered into the spirit of the occasion with the hearty zest of boys out holidaying. They were a little careful about not being too free with their spending-money. "'Cause we're out on a long run, you know," Old Tilly said. But what they did spend went for their share of the entertainment given so freely to them by the big Granger who had taken them in tow. It was a day filled with a round of pleasure, as Jot had predicted.

The athletic contests on the primitive little race-track proved the greatest attraction of all. There were bicycle races after the foot-racing and hammer-throwing and high jumping. Jot longed to vault into his own wheel and whirl round the track dizzily, like the rest of them. He and Kent stood together close to the turning-point. They had somehow drifted away from Old Tilly.

A new race began, and up at the starting-place there seemed to be a good deal of hilarity. The hearty laughs were tantalizing.

"What is it? Why don't they come on and give us fellows a chance to laugh, too?" exclaimed Jot, impatiently.

Kent was peering sharply between his hands. He suddenly began to laugh.

"It's a slow race!" he cried. "They're trying to see who can get behind! Come on up further where we can see. It'll be great!"

"Come along, then--hurry!" shouted Jot.

"It's a free-for-all. Anybody can compete," somebody was saying as they passed. "But they've got to be slower than Old Tilly!"

"Can't do it!" whispered Jot. "Old Tilly can sit still on his bike."

"I hope he'll see the race," Kent panted. "It would be mean if he missed. Here's a good place--there they come. Look at 'em crawling along like snails! There's one chap clear behind. Yes, sir, he's standing still!"

Jot gave one look and uttered a shout:

"It's Old Tilly!"

"Jotham Eddy--no!"

"Look for yourself and see--ain't it?"

"Of course--no--yes, sir, it's Old Till, for a fact."

"And he's 'way behind--I told you there wasn't anybody slower'n Old Tilly! He's beating as fast as anything."

"As slow as anything. Come on! Let's cheer him, Jot."

They caught off their caps and cheered wildly. Every-body else joined in, catching at the name and laughing over it as a good joke.

"Hurrah--hurrah for Old Tilly!"

"Hip, hip, 'n' a tiger for Old Til-ly!"

The time-keeper called time, and Old Tilly descended from his victorious wheel and bowed profoundly to his cheerers. He walked away to join the other boys with the exaggerated air of a great victor, and the people shouted again.

"Oh, I say, that was rich, Old Till," gasped Jot. "That was worth a farm!"

"What made you think of entering?" Kent laughed.

"Oh, I thought I would--I knew I could beat 'em," Old Tilly said modestly.

Sunset ended the festivities in the grove, and the boys mounted and rode away with the other tired people. Gradually they fell behind.

"Don't--rush--so; I've got to keep up my reputation!" said Old Tilly. "Besides, I'm tired."

"Me, too."

"Same here. Let's camp out to-night in the woods. Why didn't we stay there and camp in that grove?"

"Well, we might have, but we won't go back," answered Old Tilly. "Come on, let's make for that pretty little brown house. Maybe we can buy our supper there."

But the little brown house was shut up tight. The curtains were all pulled down, and a general air of "not at home" pervaded even the clapboards and the morning-glory vine over the door. Only the neat little barn looked hospitable. Its doors stood open wide. A distant rumble of thunder suddenly sounded, and the sky darkened with ominous swiftness.

"Going to rain," Kent said.

"Sure," added Jot. "Look at those clouds, will you? We'd better get into a hole somewhere."

"We'll go into the barn," decided Old Tilly, after a minute's thought, "and if it rains all night, we'll stay there. We can't do any harm."

It rained all night. Shower after shower burst over them heavily, and there was a continual boom of thunder in their ears. A slight respite at midnight was followed by the most terrific shower of all. The boys huddled together in the hay, with awe-struck faces, but unafraid. They could not sleep in such a magnificent tumult of nature.

Suddenly there was a blinding flash of lightning, then a crash. The whole universe seemed tottering about them. Dizzy and stunned, they gazed at each other, unable to move for an instant. Then it was Jot who sprang up in tremulous haste.

"I smell smoke--we're afire!" he exclaimed.

"Yes," Old Tilly cried, striving to be calm, "it struck this barn."

CHAPTER VII.

They darted away in search of the fire. The glare of the lightning showed them their way, and presently they came into the glare of the flames. The bolt had descended through the harness room.

"Quick! Cattle first!" shouted Old Tilly, clearly. "We must save the cattle, anyway!"

"You go to them, you two--I'm going to the pump," called back Kent, decisively. He remembered there was a pump just outside the barn, and he was sure he had seen two or three pails standing about near it--yes, there they were! He caught them up with a sweep as he leaped by. It was the work of a moment to fill two pails and a moment more to dash them down by the floor in one corner where the scattered hay was burning. Again and again he made flying leaps to the pump and back.

Meanwhile the other two boys were releasing the frantic cattle. It was no simple thing to do--the poor creatures were so terrified. There were two steers and a gentle-faced heifer. The boys had made acquaintance with them the night before, and the poor things greeted them now with piteous lows of appeal.

"So, boss--so boss--so-o!" soothed Jot at the heifer's head. His trembling fingers caressed the smooth, fawn-colored nose, as, with the other hand, he untied her. She crouched back at first and refused to pass that terrible flaming something on the way to safety outside. But Jot pulled her along, talking to her all the way.

In less time than it takes to tell of it, the cattle were out of danger.

"Now the hens--hurry, hurry, Jot! I'm going to help Kent. It mustn't get to the hay upstairs!"

Thanks to Kent's steady, tireless work, there was little danger of that now. Already the flames were greatly subdued, and only sputtered aimlessly under the regular showers of water that fell upon them. The two boys toiled over them patiently till just a blackened corner told that they had been there in the trig little barn.

It had been a short, sharp battle. A moment's indecision, a very little less determined effort and presence of mind, and nothing but a miracle could have saved the barn. And then the house! It stood so near--what could have saved it?

It was an hour or more before Old Tilly would allow the live stock brought back into the barn. They hovered anxiously over the blackened embers, for fear they might spring into life again. But at last there seemed no danger, and presently the building settled back to quiet again, and the tired rescuers tried to snatch a little sleep in the hay. Jot woke the others in the first dim daylight.

"Fire! Fire!" he screamed.

"Where? Where is it?" cried Kent, springing to his feet.

"Put--it--o-ut," mumbled Old Tilly.

It was only a nightmare, but the boys could not doze again after it.

It was just as the sun was rising clear and beautiful that the boys came out from the barn, and as they caught sight of each other's blackened faces in the dazzling light, they each gave way to a roar of laughter. "Well, we all seem to be in the same boat," said Kent, making for the pump and filling the pails one after the other. "Here's a pail apiece; that ought to do it for us." Then he went to one of the wheel baskets and brought back a crash towel and a generous piece of soap. "Now lay to on yourselves, boys, and then we will see what we can scare up for breakfast. I suppose there's no getting into the house, so we'll have to depend on ourselves." But here Kent noticed how particularly quiet Old Tilly was.

"What's up, lad?" he said, as he plunged his face down into one of the dripping pails, and then after scrubbing and sputtering for a while he reached out blindly for a, towel, which one of the others tossed into his hands. When his eyes were free, he drew a long breath, saying, "Water fixes a fellow all right." But as he did this he noticed something that made him exclaim sharply. It was the sight of Old Tilly washing himself with one hand, while around the wrist of the other a grimy handkerchief was bound. "Why didn't you say you were hurt?" he said, coming over to Old Tilly's side. "What is it, anyway?"

"Oh, it's nothing," said Old Tilly, with an impatient nod of his head. "Maybe it's where the lightning ran down," he said, with a laugh.

"Lightning!--not much! Come, out with it. What is it?"

"Oh, it's just a tear on an old nail. One of those steers got a little ugly, and I jumped back too suddenly. It's nothing."

"We'll have to take your word for it," said Kent. But he very soberly turned to the lunch baskets. It was just as they had packed up everything neatly and were mounting their wheels to ride away, that a wagon came rumbling down the grassy road and turned in to the farmyard. A young man with a limp felt hat was on the seat with a woman wearing a brown straw hat, while a tiny girl in a pink sunbonnet was nestled down between them.

"Halloo!" said the man, as he saw the boys. "Just leavin'?"

"Yes, sir," said Old Tilly, respectfully. "We took the liberty of sleeping in your barn last night. You see the storm kept us there all night."

"Well, the storm kept us, too," said the young farmer, reaching for the little child and setting her down by the pump, and then helping the woman to alight.

The young woman gave a relieved look around, first at the barn and then at the house, and said delightedly:

"Oh, Jim, how good it does seem to see everything safe! I can't believe my eyes hardly." And she added, turning to the boys with a slightly embarrassed laugh, "I never was very good to stay away from home nights, and we didn't mean to stay last night, but the rain kept us. It just seemed to me that with every clap of thunder we'd find everything burned to ashes, and the whole place gone."

Tears came into her eyes, as she turned and gave her hand to the little child. "Well, I'm going in to get breakfast," she said, a glad, tremulous light showing across her face. "You better bring these boys in to breakfast, Jim. If they've just slept in the barn they must be hungry." Then turning back again with a heartier laugh, "I feel that glad to see everything, even to the chickens, just as we left them, that I wouldn't object to asking the President of the United States to breakfast. You ain't from around here, are you?" she asked, looking at the boys. "I thought not. And you're hungry, I'll wager," she said, as she bustled away with the little girl tugging at her skirts, not waiting for the boys to disaffirm, as they most assuredly would have done had a chance been given them, for they were not in the least hungry. But then, what was a cold luncheon taken from a bicycle basket compared with a warm breakfast that might include ham and eggs?

"She's awfully nervous, Nancy is," said the young farmer, a trifle apologetically; "she would have it at brother Ed's that she was being burned out of house and home. We oughtn't to have stayed, but brother Ed urged us to go home with him. She's always that way when she's away. We've ridden nineteen miles since daybreak, and she believed every mile that we were going to see a burned-down house at the end."

"Well," said Old Tilly in a quiet way, so as not to alarm the young farmer, "I guess she was about right this time. If we hadn't happened here--" Then he slipped back into the barn, and the young farmer followed after, and Old Tilly pointed to the blackened corner, while the other two drew near interestedly.

"You see how it struck," Old Tilly said quietly, "but we put it out after a while. It is well we happened to be right here."

The young farmer was gazing at the burned place, with his jaw dropped and a look of terror coming into his blue eyes.

"It did strike! I should say it did!" he cried excitedly. "What will Nancy say?"

[Illustration: "I should say it did strike!" he cried, excitedly.]

Then as a realization came to him that it was owing to the boys that they had a roof over their heads, he turned first to one lad and then to the other, and shook their hands heartily. There were tears in his eyes, but he did not seem conscious of them. "I don't know what Nancy 'll say," he reiterated, as he shook one hand after the other up and down like a pump handle. "We'll have to be everlastingly obliged to you for the rest of our days," he said, trying to laugh a little. But his voice choked, and he turned away to hide his emotion. Then he dropped down upon a corn-cutter and insisted on hearing the story from beginning to end, although Old Tilly declared time and again, with the other two joining in, that "It was nothing."

"You call it nothing? Well, you wait until you've worked half a lifetime, as Nancy and me have done, to get a place, and then see what you think about it. I guess Nancy 'll believe it's something."

Then he stopped as a clear call, "Breakfast! Breakfast!" came ringing out to them from the open door beyond the pump. "Perhaps we'd better not say anything about it until after breakfast. She's had a powerful uneasy night, and it's been a good bit of a ride over, too."

To this the boys assented, and the four walked across the yard to the kitchen door, where the little girl was shyly waiting for them.

"Ain't you the young chap that beat in the bicycle slow race?" asked Nancy, when she caught a sight of Tilly's face as he removed his hat.

The other two boys laughed, and the farmer, looking squarely at his visitor, said:

"Well, I thought I'd seen you somewhere."

And then they settled down to breakfast in the happiest frame of mind, evidently, that could be imagined. But all the time Old Tilly kept one hand down at his side, a little out of sight, and the boys noticed that he took upon his plate only such things as he could very easily manage with one hand. The breakfast, for a hurried one, was very satisfactory indeed. Jot and Kent ate with full appreciation of it.

But had they watched closely, they would have seen how Old Tilly's face now flushed and then grew pale, and that occasionally he brought his lips together as though striving to control himself.

But, all unmindful of what the boy was undergoing, Nancy presided merrily over the table, and kept prompting Jim to fill up the plates as they needed it, and pressed this and that upon the boys' attention.

"I don't feel as if I should ever want to go away again," she cried. "It's so good to be at home. I've been through every room in the house and taken a view of them all." And then she said laughingly, turning to the boys, "Not that there are so very many of 'em, but they're all we've got, you know. After breakfast we're going out to the barn, ain't we, Polly?" she added.

But now Kent noticed that Jot's face had suddenly sobered; he was looking at Old Tilly anxiously; he had seen. His hand come up from beneath the table, and he was sure that the handkerchief was spotted with red. "I say--Old Tilly--" Jot got to his feet hastily.

But Old Tilly's face was white, and he was swaying from side to side. Old Tilly was fainting away.

CHAPTER VIII.

I--I'm awake now. What's the matter? Who's sick?"
Old Tilly sat up dizzily. He had lost consciousness only for a moment, but his
face seemed to be growing whiter and whiter. Jot and Kent hovered over him
anxiously.

"You got kind of faint, Old Till--just for a minute. You're all right now," Kent
said.

"Of course I'm all right!--I always was! I don't see what you're making such a
fuss about!" But the pale face belied his words.

Kent lifted the clumsily bandaged hand and unwound the handkerchief. It was
stained with blood.

"Oh, what have you done, Kent! You shouldn't have taken the bandage off!"
exclaimed Jot, in fright. "See how the blood is dripping from the cloth!"

"It's nothing, I tell you!" growled Old Tilly. "Wind the thing up again! It's only
a nail tear!"

Old Tilly was swaying again, and they forced him gently back. The little woman looked up startled.

"What is it, Jim? How did it happen?" she quavered.

Jim's face looked very sober. "I guess I better fetch the doctor," he said. "He
hurt it on a nail, he says. I won't stop to harness up--Old Betty's used to bein' rode
bareback."

He hurried away, followed by his wife. Jot was examining the torn wrist ten-
derly. Some new, untried strength seemed to spring into the brown, boyish face. It
took on the lines of a man's.

"It's an artery, Kentie. I know, because the blood leaps up so when the handkerchief is off. It can't have been bleeding all night. I don't understand."

"It bled some last night," said Old Tilly, "but I stopped it. I guess I hit it some-way just now against the table. It began again worse than ever. Cover it up, can't you? It's--all--right!"

"It isn't all right! Get me a little stick, quick, Kentie! No, that fork'll do. Hand it here. This bleeding's got to stop."

It seemed odd that it should be Jot--little, wild, scatter-brained Jot-- who should take the lead in that calm, determined way. What had come to the boy? With pale face and set teeth he quietly bound the handkerchief tightly above the wrist, and, inserting the fork handle in the knot, twisted it about. The bleeding lessened--stopped.

"There! Now, if I keep a good grip on it--oh, I say, Kentie, wasn't I afraid I couldn't work it!" he said, breathing hard.

"I don't see how you did work it! I don't see how you ever thought of it, Jot Eddy!"

"Well, I did. I read how it was done, up in the consultery. Father may laugh, but I'm going to be a doctor!"

Kent's face was full of new-born respect. He suddenly remembered that it was Jot who had set "Rover's broken leg and nursed the little sick calf that father set such store by.

"I guess father won't laugh." Kent said soberly. Jot was sitting on the edge of the lounge holding the fork in a firm grasp.   Old Tilly opened his eyes and nodded approvingly.

"That's what I tried to do myself with the handkerchief--bind it tight. It wasn't very bad at first, but I jerked it or something. I didn't want you fellows' good time spoiled."

"That's just like you!" burst out Kent. "You never tell when you get hurt, for fear other folks'll be bothered."

The little woman crept back into the kitchen and went quietly about her work.

The doctor soon came, and in a brief time the artery was taken up and the hand deftly bandaged.

"Which of you fellows made that tourniquet with the fork?" the doctor asked brusquely.

Kent pointed proudly to Jot.

"Oh, it was you, was it? Well, you did a mighty good thing for your brother there. He'd have lost plenty of blood before I got here if you hadn't."

The whole of that day and the next night the boys remained at "Jim's." The doctor had positively objected to Old Tilly's going on without a day's quiet.

And the little woman--the little woman would not hear of anything else but their staying! She had been out to the barn with Jim and seen the blackened corner. After that she hovered over the three boys like a hen over her chickens.

"For--to think, Jim!--it was saving our home he got hurt!" she cried.

The boys talked things over together, and Kent and Jot were for turning about and going straight home. But not so Old Tilly.

"I guess! No, sir; we'll go right ahead and have our holiday out. It's great fun cruising round like this!"

"But your hand, Old Tilly--the doctor said--"

"To keep it quiet. He didn't say to sit down in a rocking-chair and sing it to sleep. I guess if I can't ride a wheel with one hand, my name isn't Nathan Eddy!"

"It isn't'" laughed Kent. "It's Old Tilly Eddy!"

But in the middle of the night a ghost appeared suddenly over Old Tilly. The pale moonlight introduced it timidly as Jot, in his white shirt. He sat down on the bed.

"I'm going home," he announced in a whisper. "You other fellows can do as you like. Of course you can ride all right with one hand, if you're bound to. But I sha'n't ride with three hands any further from home! I'm going home! I--I feel as if I must!"

Old Tilly sat up in bed. "You sick, Jotham Eddy?" he cried.

"No--o, not sick--not reg'lar built! But I tell you I'm going home. It's no use saying anything--I've said it." "I believe you're sick; you're keeping something back, Jot."

"Well, what if I am? Didn't you keep something back yourself, till you fainted away doing it? I'm going--you and Kentie needn't, of course. I tell you I feel as if I must."

"He's sick, Kentie," Old Tilly said next morning. "There's something the matter with him, sure, or he wouldn't be so set. Don't you think he LOOKS kind of pale-ish?"

"Pale-ish!" scoffed Kent.

"Well, something's up. Mother put him in my care, and I'm going to take him home. I'd never forgive myself, and mother'd never forgive me, if anything happened to Jot away from home. I'm sorry on your account, Kentie."

"Oh, go ahead! I'm all right," rejoined Kent, cheerfully. "I'd just as soon. We've had a jolly good time of it so far, and we can take the rest of it out in going fishing or camping at home."

"Well, then we'll go right back home--on Jot's account. I feet as if I must take him to mother."

Poor Jot! It was hard to be taken home that way, when all the while wasn't he taking wounded Old Tilly home to mother? It was the only way he had been able to work it out, lying awake and worrying over the torn wrist. Something must be done to get Old Tilly home.

"I told the truth--I said I was keeping something back," thought Jot. "I said I wasn't sick, didn't I? And Old Till's got to go home. The doctor told me the sooner the better."

But it was a distinct sacrifice to Jot's pride to be "taken home to mother." He bore it remarkably well because of the love and anxiety in his sturdy little heart. He would do a good deal for Old Till.

They returned by a more direct route than they had come. On the way, they discussed their adventures. Jot counted them up on his fingers.

"Hand-organs, old churches, little old man's hay--pshaw! that wasn't an adventure!" Jot blushed hotly, as if caught in some misdeed.

"No, skip that," Old Tilly said quietly. "That just happened. Begin over again."

"Hand-organs, old churches (two adventures there, you know), picnics, slow races--"

"Skip that!" cried Old Tilly.

"No, sir! Slow races, burning barns, arteries--" "Oh, I say! I'll do the counting up myself! Besides, you left out the very first adventure, didn't you?"

"The very first one?"

"Yes, of course--losing all our money before we started!"

"Quits!" cried Jot, laughing. He did not appear sick at all. All the way home he watched Old Tilly with almost professional care. And Old Tilly, unknown to Jot, watched him.

"Say, Jot," he said that night, when they had gone upstairs to their own beds once more, "don't you feel a little better?" His face was white and tired, and he nestled in the pillows gratefully. It was good to be at home. "Don't you feel a good deal better?"

"Me?" asked innocent Jot. "I feel jolly! Never felt--oh, er--I mean-- that is--"

"You're a rascal!" laughed Old Tilly, comfortably. "That's what you mean. Think I didn't surmise a thing or two? Well, honest, I didn't, at first. But on the way home I found out what you were up to. You looked altogether too healthy!"

There was a moment's silence, then Jot spoke meekly. "I felt sort of mean, but I couldn't help it, honest. And I told the truth, now, didn't I? I was going to own up to-morrow."

He went away into the next room and crept into bed beside Kent.

"Jot! Jot, I say!" called Old Tilly, presently. "Hope you don't think I'm mad. I don't mind. I--I like it."

There was an indistinct mumble of relief from Jot's quarter, followed by another silence. Then again Old Tilly's contented voice crept through the dark.

"Say, Jot, you asleep?"

"Yes, you?"

"Sound! It feels mighty good to be home, doesn't it?"

"Prime!"

"Good-night, old chap!"

"Same here!"

Then silence, unbroken. By and by Mother Eddy stole upstairs to her boys.

"Good boys, every one of them. God bless them!" she murmured. "Home isn't home without them. But young things must have their holidaying. And I guess from what they tell, they've made good use of theirs. And it isn't everyone does that; some of them just waste it. But this one's held something in it. I don't know just what. But every one of them seems--well, sort o' more manly-like. I'm glad their pa let them go. But home ain't home without boys in it. That's sure."

And she turned and went softly down the stairs.

The Codes Of Hammurabi And Moses
W. W. Davies

QTY

The discovery of the Hammurabi Code is one of the greatest achievements of archaeology, and is of paramount interest, not only to the student of the Bible, but also to all those interested in ancient history...

Religion   **ISBN: *1-59462-338-4***   **Pages:132**
MSRP $12.95

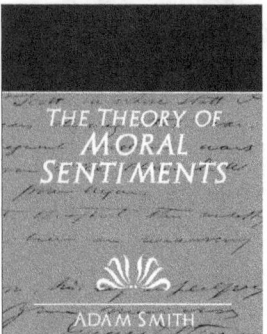

The Theory of Moral Sentiments
Adam Smith

QTY

This work from 1749. contains original theories of conscience amd moral judgment and it is the foundation for systemof morals.

Philosophy **ISBN: *1-59462-777-0***   **Pages:536**
MSRP $19.95

Jessica's First Prayer
Hesba Stretton

QTY

In a screened and secluded corner of one of the many railway-bridges which span the streets of London there could be seen a few years ago, from five o'clock every morning until half past eight, a tidily set-out coffee-stall, consisting of a trestle and board, upon which stood two large tin cans, with a small fire of charcoal burning under each so as to keep the coffee boiling during the early hours of the morning when the work-people were thronging into the city on their way to their daily toil...

Childrens   **ISBN: *1-59462-373-2***   **Pages:84**
MSRP $9.95

My Life and Work
Henry Ford

QTY

Henry Ford revolutionized the world with his implementation of mass production for the Model T automobile. Gain valuable business insight into his life and work with his own auto-biography... "We have only started on our development of our country we have not as yet, with all our talk of wonderful progress, done more than scratch the surface. The progress has been wonderful enough but..."

Biographies/ **ISBN: *1-59462-198-5***   **Pages:300**
MSRP $21.95

The Art of Cross-Examination
Francis Wellman

QTY

I presume it is the experience of every author, after his first book is published upon an important subject, to be almost overwhelmed with a wealth of ideas and illustrations which could readily have been included in his book, and which to his own mind, at least, seem to make a second edition inevitable. Such certainly was the case with me; and when the first edition had reached its sixth impression in five months, I rejoiced to learn that it seemed to my publishers that the book had met with a sufficiently favorable reception to justify a second and considerably enlarged edition. ..

Pages:412

Reference   ISBN: *1-59462-647-2*   *MSRP $19.95*

On the Duty of Civil Disobedience
Henry David Thoreau

QTY

Thoreau wrote his famous essay, On the Duty of Civil Disobedience, as a protest against an unjust but popular war and the immoral but popular institution of slave-owning. He did more than write—he declined to pay his taxes, and was hauled off to gaol in consequence. Who can say how much this refusal of his hastened the end of the war and of slavery ?

Law   ISBN: *1-59462-747-9*   **Pages:48**
                                        MSRP $7.45

Dream Psychology Psychoanalysis for Beginners
Sigmund Freud

QTY

Sigmund Freud, born Sigismund Schlomo Freud (May 6, 1856 - September 23, 1939), was a Jewish-Austrian neurologist and psychiatrist who co-founded the psychoanalytic school of psychology. Freud is best known for his theories of the unconscious mind, especially involving the mechanism of repression; his redefinition of sexual desire as mobile and directed towards a wide variety of objects; and his therapeutic techniques, especially his understanding of transference in the therapeutic relationship and the presumed value of dreams as sources of insight into unconscious desires.

Pages:196

Psychology   ISBN: *1-59462-905-6*   *MSRP $15.45*

The Miracle of Right Thought
Orison Swett Marden

QTY

Believe with all of your heart that you will do what you were made to do. When the mind has once formed the habit of holding cheerful, happy, prosperous pictures, it will not be easy to form the opposite habit. It does not matter how improbable or how far away this realization may see, or how dark the prospects may be, if we visualize them as best we can, as vividly as possible, hold tenaciously to them and vigorously struggle to attain them, they will gradually become actualized, realized in the life. But a desire, a longing without endeavor, a yearning abandoned or held indifferently will vanish without realization.

Pages:360

Self Help   ISBN: *1-59462-644-8*   *MSRP $25.45*

QTY

The Rosicrucian Cosmo-Conception Mystic Christianity *by Max Heindel*   ISBN: 1-59462-188-8   **$38.95**
The Rosicrucian Cosmo-conception is not dogmatic, neither does it appeal to any other authority than the reason of the student. It is: not controversial, but is: sent forth in the, hope that it may help to clear...   New Age/Religion Pages 646

Abandonment To Divine Providence *by Jean-Pierre de Caussade*   ISBN: 1-59462-228-0   **$25.95**
"The Rev. Jean Pierre de Caussade was one of the most remarkable spiritual writers of the Society of Jesus in France in the 18th Century. His death took place at Toulouse in 1751. His works have gone through many editions and have been republished...   Inspirational/Religion Pages 400

Mental Chemistry *by Charles Haanel*   ISBN: 1-59462-192-6   **$23.95**
Mental Chemistry allows the change of material conditions by combining and appropriately utilizing the power of the mind. Much like applied chemistry creates something new and unique out of careful combinations of chemicals the mastery of mental chemistry...   New Age Pages 354

The Letters of Robert Browning and Elizabeth Barret Barrett 1845-1846 vol II   ISBN: 1-59462-193-4   **$35.95**
by Robert Browning and Elizabeth Barrett   Biographies Pages 596

Gleanings In Genesis (volume I) *by Arthur W. Pink*   ISBN: 1-59462-130-6   **$27.45**
Appropriately has Genesis been termed "the seed plot of the Bible" for in it we have, in germ form, almost all of the great doctrines which are afterwards fully developed in the books of Scripture which follow...   Religion/Inspirational Pages 420

The Master Key *by L. W. de Laurence*   ISBN: 1-59462-001-6   **$30.95**
In no branch of human knowledge has there been a more lively increase of the spirit of research during the past few years than in the study of Psychology, Concentration and Mental Discipline. The requests for authentic lessons in Thought Control, Mental Discipline and...   New Age/Business Pages 422

The Lesser Key Of Solomon Goetia *by L. W. de Laurence*   ISBN: 1-59462-092-X   **$9.95**
This translation of the first book of the "Lemegton" which is now for the first time made accessible to students of Talismanic Magic was done, after careful collation and edition, from numerous Ancient Manuscripts in Hebrew, Latin, and French...   New Age/Occult Pages 92

Rubaiyat Of Omar Khayyam *by Edward Fitzgerald*   ISBN:1-59462-332-5   **$13.95**
Edward Fitzgerald, whom the world has already learned, in spite of his own efforts to look within the shadow of anonymity, to look upon as one of the rarest poets of the century, was born at Bredfield, in Suffolk, on the 31st of March, 1809. He was the third son of John Purcell...   Music Pages 172

Ancient Law *by Henry Maine*   ISBN: 1-59462-128-4   **$29.95**
The chief object of the following pages is to indicate some of the earliest ideas of mankind, as they are reflected in Ancient Law, and to point out the relation of those ideas to modern thought.   Religiom/History Pages 452

Far-Away Stories *by William J. Locke*   ISBN: 1-59462-129-2   **$19.45**
"Good wine needs no bush, but a collection of mixed vintages does. And this book is just such a collection. Some of the stories I do not want to remain buried for ever in the museum files of dead magazine-numbers an author's not unpardonable vanity..."   Fiction Pages 272

Life of David Crockett *by David Crockett*   ISBN: 1-59462-250-7   **$27.45**
"Colonel David Crockett was one of the most remarkable men of the times in which he lived. Born in humble life, but gifted with a strong will, an indomitable courage, and unremitting perseverance...   Biographies/New Age Pages 424

Lip-Reading *by Edward Nitchie*   ISBN: 1-59462-206-X   **$25.95**
Edward B. Nitchie, founder of the New York School for the Hard of Hearing, now the Nitchie School of Lip-Reading, Inc, wrote "LIP-READING Principles and Practice". The development and perfecting of this meritorious work on lip-reading was an undertaking...   How-to Pages 400

A Handbook of Suggestive Therapeutics, Applied Hypnotism, Psychic Science   ISBN: 1-59462-214-0   **$24.95**
by Henry Munro   Health/New Age/Health/Self-help Pages 376

A Doll's House: and Two Other Plays *by Henrik Ibsen*   ISBN: 1-59462-112-8   **$19.95**
Henrik Ibsen created this classic when in revolutionary 1848 Rome. Introducing some striking concepts in playwriting for the realist genre, this play has been studied the world over.   Fiction/Classics/Plays 308

The Light of Asia *by sir Edwin Arnold*   ISBN: 1-59462-204-3   **$13.95**
In this poetic masterpiece, Edwin Arnold describes the life and teachings of Buddha. The man who was to become known as Buddha to the world was born as Prince Gautama of India but he rejected the worldly riches and abandoned the reigns of power when...   Religion/History/Biographies Pages 170

The Complete Works of Guy de Maupassant *by Guy de Maupassant*   ISBN: 1-59462-157-8   **$16.95**
"For days and days, nights and nights, I had dreamed of that first kiss which was to consecrate our engagement, and I knew not on what spot I should put my lips..."   Fiction/Classics Pages 240

The Art of Cross-Examination *by Francis L. Wellman*   ISBN: 1-59462-309-0   **$26.95**
Written by a renowned trial lawyer, Wellman imparts his experience and uses case studies to explain how to use psychology to extract desired information through questioning.   How-to/Science/Reference Pages 408

Answered or Unanswered? *by Louisa Vaughan*   ISBN: 1-59462-248-5   **$10.95**
Miracles of Faith in China   Religion Pages 112

The Edinburgh Lectures on Mental Science (1909) *by Thomas*   ISBN: 1-59462-008-3   **$11.95**
This book contains the substance of a course of lectures recently given by the writer in the Queen Street Hail, Edinburgh. Its purpose is to indicate the Natural Principles governing the relation between Mental Action and Material Conditions...   New Age/Psychology Pages 148

Ayesha *by H. Rider Haggard*   ISBN: 1-59462-301-5   **$24.95**
Verily and indeed it is the unexpected that happens! Probably if there was one person upon the earth from whom the Editor of this, and of a certain previous history, did not expect to hear again...   Classics Pages 380

Ayala's Angel *by Anthony Trollope*   ISBN: 1-59462-352-X   **$29.95**
The two girls were both pretty, but Lucy who was twenty-one who supposed to be simple and comparatively unattractive, whereas Ayala was credited, as her Bombwhat romantic name might show, with poetic charm and a taste for romance. Ayala when her father died was nineteen...   Fiction Pages 484

The American Commonwealth *by James Bryce*   ISBN: 1-59462-286-8   **$34.45**
An interpretation of American democratic political theory. It examines political mechanics and society from the perspective of Scotsman James Bryce   Politics Pages 572

Stories of the Pilgrims *by Margaret P. Pumphrey*   ISBN: 1-59462-116-0   **$17.95**
This book explores pilgrims religious oppression in England as well as their escape to Holland and eventual crossing to America on the Mayflower, and their early days in New England...   History Pages 268

www.bookjungle.com *email: sales@bookjungle.com fax: 630-214-0564 mail: Book Jungle PO Box 2226 Champaign, IL 61825*

QTY

The Fasting Cure *by Sinclair Upton*   ISBN: *1-59462-222-1*   **$13.95**

In the Cosmopolitan Magazine for May, 1910, and in the Contemporary Review (London) for April, 1910, I published an article dealing with my experi-
ences in fasting. I have written a great many magazine articles, but never one which attracted so much attention... New Age/Self Help/Health Pages 164

Hebrew Astrology *by Sepharial*   ISBN: *1-59462-308-2*   **$13.45**

In these days of advanced thinking it is a matter of common observation that we have left many of the old landmarks behind and that we are now pressing
forward to greater heights and to a wider horizon than that which represented the mind-content of our progenitors...   Astrology Pages 144

Thought Vibration or The Law of Attraction in the Thought World   ISBN: *1-59462-127-6*   **$12.95**

by William Walker Atkinson   *Psychology/Religion Pages 144*

Optimism *by Helen Keller*   ISBN: *1-59462-108-X*   **$15.95**

Helen Keller was blind, deaf, and mute since 19 months old, yet famously learned how to overcome these handicaps, communicate with the world, and
spread her lectures promoting optimism. An inspiring read for everyone...   Biographies/Inspirational Pages 84

Sara Crewe *by Frances Burnett*   ISBN: *1-59462-360-0*   **$9.45**

In the first place, Miss Minchin lived in London. Her home was a large, dull, tall one, in a large, dull square, where all the houses were alike, and all the
sparrows were alike, and where all the door-knockers made the same heavy sound...   Childrens/Classic Pages 88

The Autobiography of Benjamin Franklin *by Benjamin Franklin*   ISBN: *1-59462-135-7*   **$24.95**

The Autobiography of Benjamin Franklin has probably been more extensively read than any other American historical work, and no other book of its kind
has had such ups and downs of fortune. Franklin lived for many years in England, where he was agent...   Biographies/History Pages 332

Name	
Email	
Telephone	
Address	
City, State ZIP	

☐ Credit Card   ☐ Check / Money Order

Credit Card Number	
Expiration Date	
Signature	

Please Mail to: Book Jungle
PO Box 2226
Champaign, IL 61825
or Fax to: 630-214-0564

ORDERING INFORMATION

web*: www.bookjungle.com*
email*: sales@bookjungle.com*
fax*: 630-214-0564*
mail*: Book Jungle PO Box 2226 Champaign, IL 61825*
or PayPal *to sales@bookjungle.com*

Please contact us for bulk discounts

DIRECT-ORDER TERMS

20% Discount if You Order
Two or More Books
Free Domestic Shipping!
Accepted: Master Card, Visa,
Discover, American Express